An Elephant's Story

Written & Illustrated
By:
Jamie Renee Heraver

Acknowledgements

To my mom, who is my biggest fan- thank you for supporting this book and all that I do.

To Steve, my friend and graphic designer- I couldn't have done this without you. Thank you for the many hours you've spent working on this project from the kindness of your heart.

To Matt, my friend, talented artist, and voice for the elephants- thank you for mentoring me in art, encouraging me to follow my dreams, and inspiring me to pursue this passion outside of my comfort zone.

To all of you who are a voice for animals, working behind the scenes, dedicating endless hours to rescue and the humane treatment of animals- you are my inspiration daily.

To John, my neighbor and friend- thank you for taking your time to teach me Illustrator.

To all of my family and close friends who have been alongside me throughout this process, encouraging me and building me up- your support means the world to me.

A portion of the proceeds from this book will be donated to GFAS accredited sanctuaries.

———

Published by Jamie Renee Heraver
P.O. Box 16
Huntington Beach, CA 92648

ISBN-13: 978-0692158302
ISBN-10: 0692158308

Library of Congress Control Number: 2018908719

Visit www.endanimalslavery.net to learn more about Jamie's books and how to help animals.

Printed in the United States of America.

Graphic Designer: Steve Martin

This book is dedicated to Paula,

a working elephant.

The eyes of an animal are windows to God's
love. We all should listen to their silent words.

-Jim Gould

One special day when the sun shined bright,

stood a girl and an elephant

on a hill in plain sight.

She looked in his eyes,

and he looked in hers.

Then all of a sudden,

she could see two tears.

She could feel his heart

and hear the thoughts in his mind.

He told her a story all about

his kind.

I was rubbing my trunk on a tree

just for fun

when I heard a loud

BANG,

and I started to RUN!

It happened so fast

with a rope and a knot.

I was taken away

from my muddy green lot.

I cried for my mom.
I yelled,
and I begged.

But the longer
I tried,
the further they legged.

Minutes

Turned to hours

and

hours to a

day.

We arrived at a place

with cement,

walls,

and hay.

They yelled, and they poked

a sharp hook in my ears.

I cried, and I screamed

'til I ran out of tears.

I finally gave up
and fell to the ground,
and then it was time
for the training to abound.

With that long metal hook
that I'll never forget,
they taught me their words
and how to paint a silhouette.

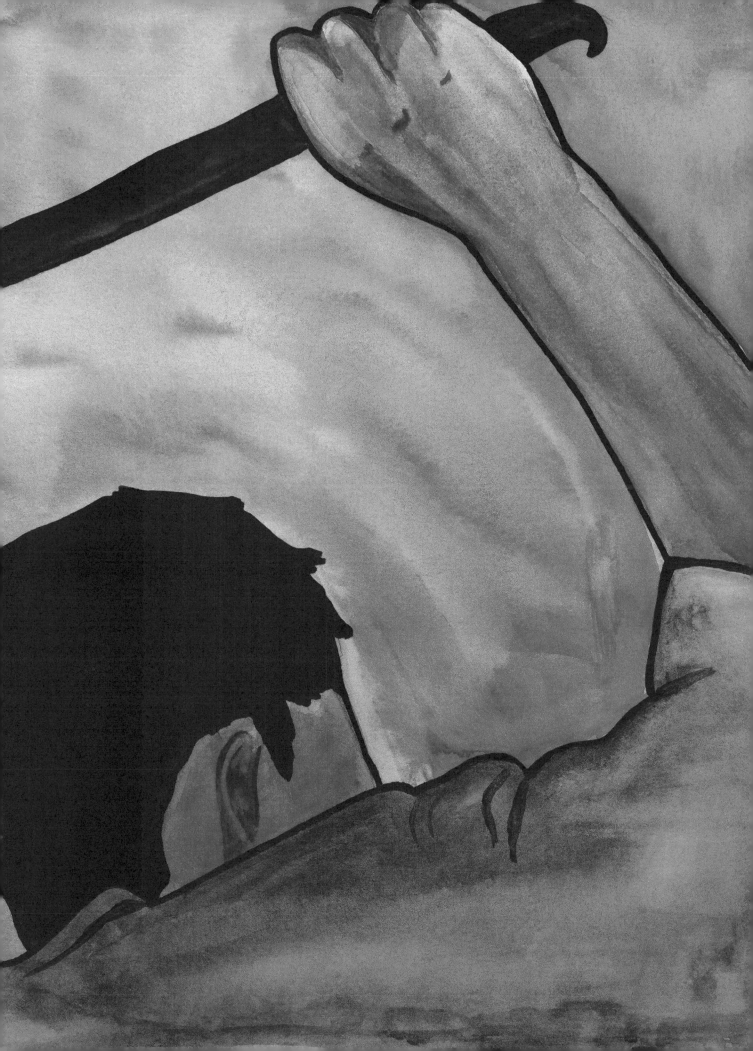

The tourists will love it!

Make him draw! Make him paint!

I worked for long hours

'til I wanted to faint.

My heart was so sad,

and I missed my herd.

But I had to paint

by a poke and a word.

Hours
turned to days,
and
days turned to
Years.

Then a man

with a truck came

and

rattled my

fears.

He came **from a camp**
with a large
square **crate.**

This new adventure
made me wonder
my **fate.**

After a long trip
that felt like a day,
I couldn't wait to come out
for a walk and some hay.

I looked all around
after I finished my snack
and saw elephants
I KNEW with people
on their back!

With that long metal hook
that I'll never forget,

I learned
to give rides from sunrise
to sunset.

I remembered the days
on the grasses and plains,

peaceful and happy
without any chains.

Hours
turned to days,
and
days turned to
years.
Then a man and a woman
came
with special careers.
They rescued elephants
who'd been through a lot
and
took them to places
where their pain would be
forgot.

That's why I'm here now
with my new family.
In my heart and my mind,
I feel happy and free!

The girl looked in his eyes,

and he looked in hers.

All of a sudden,

he could see two tears.

He pulled her close and said,

don't be sad.

All that is over,

and

now I am GLAD!

Let the joy you feel now
fill your heart
and your ears.

Show respect
and LOVE to us
all of your years.

We all have a place
we belong to be,
and
now you have
the power
to be a
VOICE FOR ME.

Did you know?

Elephants are the largest and most intelligent land animals. They have 3 times as many neurons as humans, can weigh between 5,000-14,000 pounds, and can live up to 70 years depending on the species.

Elephants are extremely social and form close bonds with one another. Female elephants remain in their family for a lifetime, and bulls (male elephants) leave their mothers at approximately 12 years old. It has been reported that elephants can recognize former companions after being separated for more than 20 years.

Babies remain in their mother's womb for about 22 months and can weigh up to 200 pounds at birth. They rely completely on their mother's breast milk for the first year and are completely weaned at about 3 years old.

Elephants are herbivores. They consume about 300 pounds of grass and plant material daily and can walk up to 10 miles per day to find food and water.

Over the course of many years, elephants will often recognize routes to water and food and teach their young the same routes. They can even use tools for gathering food in hard-to-reach places.

Elephants are known to be extremely emotional. They display signs of empathy such as stroking one another with their trunks and making chirping sounds during times of distress. They also mourn the loss of loved ones, often standing near the deceased body for hours and caressing the bones left behind.

The most sensitive places on an elephant are its inner ears, face, neck, trunk, and soles of its feet. The nose of an elephant is sensitive enough to pick up a blade of grass, and it will often avoid irritants like ants when gathering food.

Approximately 15,000-20,000 elephants are in captivity today. The large majority of these gentle giants are taken from the wild, used for entertainment and harsh logging work, and are used for unethical breeding practices that do not improve conservation efforts.

How Can We Help Elephants?

We can become educated about the needs of elephants and how to best support conservation efforts.

We can spread the word! Sharing what we learn with friends and family on social media can make a big difference.

We can use our skills like writing, designing, speaking, teaching, marketing, volunteering, and attending outreach events to help ethical organizations.

We can visit and donate to organizations that provide a safe haven for elephants and participate in conservation efforts, instead of purchasing tickets to circuses, elephant rides, and other places where elephants are exploited for entertainment.

We can ask for policy change by writing our local politcal leaders and attending city council meetings. They care if we do!

Resources

The David Sheldrick Wildlife Trust
www.sheldrickwildlifetrust.org

Elephant Guardians of Los Angeles
www.elephantguardians.org

Elephant Nature Park, Thailand
www.elephantnaturepark.org

The Elephant Sanctuary, TN
www.elephants.com

Elephant Voices
www.elephantvoices.org

Global Federation of Animal Sanctuaries (GFAS)
www.sanctuaryfederation.org

Global Sanctuary for Elephants, Brazil
www.globalelephants.org

One Green Planet
www.onegreenplanet.org

Performing Animal Welfare Society (PAWS), California
www.pawsweb.org

Author's Note

Summer of 2016 through Winter of 2017 were the most trying years of my life. I faced various life changing events as well as a serious injury that kept me from one of my greatest passions, surfing. Trying to cope with grief and loss, I decided to seek refuge in the presence of animals, knowing that they have a healing power unlike anything else in the world.

I soon found myself at PAWS, a beautiful sanctuary in San Andreas, CA for former performing exotic animals. For the first time, I had witnessed happy elephants in captivity where they enjoyed ample space, love, and respect. They were given the freedom to make their own decisions and engage in normal elephant behaviors I had never seen anywhere else. I began to not only discover the wonderful truths that lie in the depths of quiet animal observation, but I was also educated in the realities of the animal tourism industry. My journey to healing took on new meaning, and I knew I had to do something to make the world a better place for animals.

I continued my research, interviews, and observations at various animal atttractions. I wondered if an elephant captive to tourism and entertainment had a voice, what story would he tell? Out of that question, An Elephant's Story was birthed. I invite you to see the world behind the eyes of an elephant; and in doing so, I believe together we can make the world a better place for all on this planet.

With Love,

Jamie Renee Heraver

About the Author

Jamie Heraver was born in Waukegan, IL in 1984. She adored animals growing up and often wrote stories about them as a child. She discovered her love for art at 11 years old and began painting animal murals on walls for friends and family. Having a big heart for kids, she decided to earn her B.A. in Elementary Education in 2007 and went on to earn her M.A. in Literacy Education in 2010. After working as a Reading Specialist for 4.5 years in Illinois, she decided to pursue her dream of surfing and moved to Southern California in 2010. It was there that she reconnected with her other passions, pursuing music, art, writing, and creating while working as a private tutor. She now resides in Orange County, CA with her rescue bunny, Aloha, where she can be found dropping in on a wave, teaching some of the best kids around, and being a voice for animals.

CPSIA information can be obtained
at www.ICGtesting.com
Printed in the USA
LVHW01n2358111018
593190LV00004B/10/P